MW00345716

HUNDRED WORD HORROR

BENEATH

Compiled & edited by A.R. Ward

Hundred Word Horror: Beneath

A Ghost Orchid Press Anthology

Copyright © 2021 Ghost Orchid Press

First published in Great Britain 2021 by Ghost Orchid Press

The authors of the individual stories retain the copyright of the works featured in this anthology.

This is a work of fiction. Names, characters, places, and incidents either are the product of the author's imagination or are used fictitiously. Any resemblance to actual persons, living or dead, events, or locales is entirely coincidental.

All rights reserved. No part of this production may be reproduced, stored in a retrieval system, or transmitted in any form or by any means, electronic, recording, mechanical, photocopying or otherwise without the prior written permission of the publisher and copyright owner.

ISBN (paperback): 978-1-8383915-4-6

ISBN (e-book): 978-1-8383915-5-3

Cover design and book formatting by Claire Saag

Cover image © Karsten Winegeart via Unsplash

Illustrations from Vintage Illustrations via Canva.com

"Into the underland we have long placed that which we fear and wish to lose, and that which we love and wish to save."

—*Robert Macfarlane,* **Underland**

CONTENTS

FOREWORD

So much of horror is about "what lies beneath". From caves, to crypts, to nuclear bunkers, the possibilities are endless. This volume contains one hundred stories and poems, each of precisely one hundred words in length, by a range of both experienced and debut authors. These skilled and imaginative writers from across the globe are not afraid to look beneath the water, beneath the skin... even beneath the veneer of civilized society. What they can do in the space of one hundred words will shock, surprise, and delight you.

Happy reading!

A.R. Ward

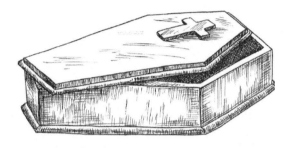

COFFINS ARE OVERRATED

1

Going Down
by Yukari Kousaka

Translated by Toshiya Kamei

I step into the elevator and press the button for the first floor. The elevator groans, shakes like a coughing old man, and goes down. The floor number on the panel slowly blinks, and I have no idea what it says. All the buttons are gone except for the emergency button. I push it hard, but no reply comes at first. Then a low voice cracks over the intercom.

"Get me out, please!" I scream. "Get me out of here!" Laughter echoes as if mocking me. I choke with tears as I cower. After an hour, I'm still going down.

Born in Osaka in 2001, YUKARI KOUSAKA is a Japanese poet, fiction writer, and essayist. Translated by Toshiya Kamei, Yukari's writings have appeared in A Story in 100 Words, The Crypt, *and* New World Writing, *among others.*

2

Grave Oversight
by E.M. Alores

Wood on four sides. Wood above and beneath. Dirt beyond in all directions. Confusion became panic. There was no bell to alert those above.

Too deep for light to penetrate, save that brilliant pop of white as one of her nails tore against the wood. Panic turned to terror. There was no path for her to escape.

The earth, an ocean, swallowed her. Terror slowly gave way to calm. There was no air left to breathe.

Sleep came easily.

Six feet above, grief was melting to acceptance. They had already wept for one death, and would never know the second.

E.M. ALORES is a California-based writer with a special love of ghosts, vampires and spooky Victorian houses. She plans to write more once she figures out how to keep her cat off the keyboard.

3

Coffins Are Overrated
by M.M. MacLeod

I heard coughing beneath my feet. Lifting the sheet of linoleum which lay atop my basement floor, I found and opened the ancient trapdoor. Surely there could be nothing below but bugs and dirt?

A metal staircase led down into a brightly lit kitchen. There was also a bed, and a tunnel leading away from the room. The cougher had fled. Who would want to live down here? I knew times were tough, but this? Then I saw the framed portrait: the white fangs and soulless eyes.

It was nighttime. I'd come back in the morning—with a wooden stake.

M.M. MACLEOD writes horror and suspense fiction, as well as poetry, in Hamilton, ON Canada. She also edits and publishes Frost Zone Zine. *@lenemacleod and @frostzonezine on Twitter.*

4

Burial
by Jessica Wilcox

"This is the last time," she said to the small box clutched in her hands.

Kneeling, she set down the box and started digging.

Moments later, her spade hit a box not unlike the one sitting next to her. *Damnit!*

Certain she hadn't used the spot, she cringed and dug another hole. Another box! *Damnit! Damnit!*

Tears flowed as hole after hole—the same thing. How could she have been this careless?

She collapsed onto the grass, bawling.

Scraping noises made her turn her head and watch as all of her little friends rose from their shallow graves, coming for her.

JESSICA WILCOX (formerly Gilmartin) hails from Buffalo, New York, where she teaches English to refugees and immigrants. She resides with her husband, three children, two cats and puppy, all of whom keep her on her toes. You can find her on most social media platforms as @jawilcox711.

5

nymphaeaceae
by doungjai gam

You stop paddling when you reach the water lilies. The largest one catches your eye—pale pink, in full bloom—and you reach for it.

Our roots quiver in gluttonous anticipation. You see the undulations underwater and watch, mesmerized.

We breach the surface and wrap around your outstretched limb, pulling you in.

Screaming is futile—no one will hear you.

You get dragged down

down

down

into the murky depths.

As we feed, another water lily begins to bloom a vivid pink.

On the land, the insects buzz frantically as the trees whisper warnings that are too late to heed.

DOUNGJAI GAM is the author of glass slipper dreams, shattered *and* watch the whole goddamned thing burn. *Born in Thailand and currently living in New England, she is slowly at work on her next project. Follow her on Twitter @djai76.*

6

Waking
by Emma Kathryn

When she opened her eyes, she foolishly thought that she was in her bed. Until she felt the wood press harshly against her back. Her hands reached up to touch more wood, this time resting above her. Palms pressed against the boards and, from between the cracks, a light sprinkling of dirt fell onto her face.

It took a moment to realise where she was. It was pitch black and the smell of earth invaded her nose. And it was cramped and cold. Oh, so cold.

She let out a wild scream and prayed that the gravedigger could hear her.

EMMA KATHRYN is a horror fanatic from Glasgow, Scotland. You can find her on Twitter @girlofgotham. When she's not scaring herself to death, she is one half of The Yearbook Committee Podcast or she's streaming indie games on Twitch. She is rather tiny and rather mad.

7

Beneath It All
by Jameson Grey

Beneath the earth, my beloved lies

No more tears, no more sighs.

Beneath her rings, a pale indent

Of love's years past, days lost in lament.

Beneath her smile—longing to be freed

For time to be gone, cruel world to take heed.

Beneath it all, scars linger unbound

A last rite in blood—wasted, then drowned.

Beneath her skin, no trace of pulse left

Wrists slashed to the bone, lifeless, bereft.

Beneath the ground, lady Lazarus lies

"No more, no more! No more!" she cries.

Beneath the wind, a knock at the door

My beloved returns, risen once more.

JAMESON GREY is originally from England but now lives with his family in western Canada. He also spent time in Asia as a child, which he understands makes him a fully-fledged third culture kid (TCK). His story "The Waiting Room" was published in The Toilet Zone: Number Two, *an anthology from Hellbound Books. He can be found online (occasionally) at jameson-grey.com and on Twitter @thejamesongrey.*

8

Together Again
by Emma Murray

I used to crawl under your covers to read by flashlight while you bit off fingernail tips, yours and mine. You fell sick; they kept me out. I'd sneak in anyway, huddle together, clammy cold. You'd just laugh and never shiver. One night, limp and pale, you wouldn't speak to me. They called me a child in hushed whispers and hid you underground.

Wielding a shovel, I push through earth, but inside the casket there's nothing except a clawed-out hole to a tunnel. I pause a moment, but then hear a giggle from far below. I'll follow you, little sister.

EMMA MURRAY has recently been published in The Broadkill Review, CC&D Magazine, *and* Literary Heist. *She spends her days taking care of her daughter and her nights writing. You can find her on Twitter @EMurrayAuthor and at emmaemurray.com.*

9

Gardening
by Fusako Ohki

Translated by Toshiya Kamei

While gardening, I nearly step on an unfamiliar bud sprouting in a corner of my yard. How odd. Even so, I decide to care for it. It grows rapidly, its leaves erupt, and soon a red flower blossoms. Every time I water the bloom, I hear my lover's voice: *I love you. I hate you. I'll never forgive you as long as I live. I love you.* Oh God, he was such a drama king. All that nagging got on my nerves. I grab a pair of shears and snip the flower as I recall my lover who lies beneath.

FUSAKO OHKI is a Japanese writer from Tokyo. She obtained her master's degree in Japanese literature from Hosei University. Her debut collection of short stories is forthcoming in 2021. Translated by Toshiya Kamei, Fusako's fiction has appeared in New World Writing.

10

The Bunker
by Meera Dandekar

The dimly lit hallways were narrow enough to spike claustrophobia. With a slight bloating in the wall, a bunker was successfully situated. Well planned under the subway station.

Marcus roamed the length of the space. One entrance, one exit. With his fingerprint constantly failing, he was sure of tampering. There was no way out.

The oxygen in the airtight room was running out. He knew he had limited time.

He struggled but the apocalyptic panic room design was foolproof.

He couldn't figure out if this was a murder attempt or his own stupidity.

The door opened as his heart stopped.

MEERA DANDEKAR loves to explore the fictional worlds that show the magical realm of being. She's studying mechanical engineering but has a definite admiration for the written word. She's currently living in Mumbai, India.

11

Claustrophilia
by Eric Raglin

The cavern embraces me

like a limestone lover,

taking my breath away

with each inch

I slither forward.

Behind me, Candy shouts,

"It's suicide!"

No, it's seduction.

Lungs crushed.

Senses deprived.

Hallucinating.

Sightless creatures

feasting on my feet,

bats sucking at my eyes.

What a delicious end.

Transcendent pleasure

nestled between

the cave's cold walls.

I shiver, not in dread,

but delight.

Candy's screaming now:

"Turn back, Ed.

Please, just come home!"

What a godawful proposition.

I say keep screaming, baby.

Scream 'til the walls

come thundering down.

We couldn't make a life together,

so let's find ecstasy in death.

ERIC RAGLIN (he/him) is a speculative fiction writer, podcaster, and horror educator from Nebraska. He frequently writes about queer issues, the terrors of capitalism, and body horror. His work has been published in Novel Noctule, Fever Dream, *and* Shiver. *Find him at ericraglin.com or on Twitter @ericraglin1992.*

12

The Serial Killer's Basement
by Colin Leonard

Mounds of upturned earth. Holes in the ground. The spade in the corner, lying against the rising damp, has a broken handle.

His father made them dig, when they were young. When they misbehaved he'd drag them down here, him and his brother, force them to dig holes, shout at them: "Sinners. Dig your graves."

Threatened he'd bury them alive.

He told me that.

Said we could pray down here together.

Some of the holes have been filled in already. Those other people are gone.

He said, "I been misbehaving again. You're a sinner too. You'd better pray with me."

COLIN LEONARD lives with his family in rural Co. Meath, Ireland, the home of the ancient Samhain festivals that spawned Halloween. His stories have been published in the magazines Dark Tales, Libbon, *and* The Harrow *and his flash fiction appears in* Lost Lore *and* Legends *from Breaking Rules Publishing.*

13

Above and Below
by Laura Shenton

The daylight hadn't left, but he had no way of being able to tell. The land above the crypt was cloaked with just a hint of dusk. Shadows from the tree branches had yet to dance across the shiny dew of the grass. The crunch of leaves as footsteps crossed them were nothing but a mystery to him. In the depths of the timeless stone chamber, he would never know who walked above him in the land of the living. The gentle breeze of the world above was nothing compared to the frigid chill of the stark loneliness down below.

The format of the Hundred Word Horror anthology speaks to LAURA SHENTON in a big way as someone who is a huge fan of Edgar Allan Poe. She will be self publishing some gothic horror novellas soon and is also a traditionally published author of several music non-fiction books.
You can find her at https://www.amazon.co.uk/s?k=Laura+Shenton

14

Wednesday Nights at the Town Cemetery
by J.R. Handfield

My mother is entombed in the mausoleum at my town's cemetery. The coroner insisted on interring her there instead of a traditional burial. In fact, Mom was already at the crypt.

"It could not wait, given the risks," the coroner said. "I trust you'll understand."

Her final resting place is easy to find. Look for the large stone structure with a thick wooden door, near the river.

Everyone with family in the crypt visits on Wednesday nights. When we hear our loved ones scratch and moan at the door, we smile, as we're sure they're telling us they love us.

J.R. HANDFIELD (@jrhandfield on Twitter) lives in Central Massachusetts with his wife, his son, and his cat; not necessarily in that order. He is a co-editor of ProleSCARYet: *Tales of Horror and Class Warfare, and his work can be found in* Hundred Word Horror: Home *from Ghost Orchid Press.*

15

Sand Crush
by Patrick Whitehurst

The weight of the dunes crushed against my thirteen-year-old spine and clawed fingers pulled at my ankles.

The air tasted wet and salty, cold in my straining lungs. When the tunnel collapsed, I hadn't reached the other end. Its entirety, big enough to army crawl, looped in a half circle through the sand dunes. A failed adventure. The cold fingers found me right after. No one heard my muffled scream. Beach sand filled my mouth, coarse and dry.

When my choked gasps came less often, I realized I would die. The clawed fingers pulled me deeper.

To my next adventure.

PATRICK WHITEHURST is the author of the novellas Monterey Noir *and* Monterey Pulp. *His fifth nonfiction book,* Murder & Mayhem in Tucson, *is scheduled for release this year. His short fiction has appeared in* Pulp Modern, Pulp Modern Flash, Switchblade Magazine, *the* Shotgun Honey *website, and elsewhere. His book reviews and author interviews can be found at* Suspense Magazine. *As a former journalist, he covered everything from the deaths of nineteen Granite Mountain Hotshots to President Barack Obama's visit to the Grand Canyon. Find him online at www.patrickwhitehurst.com or on twitter @pmwhitehurst.*

16

Fragment of an Elegy
by Clay F. Johnson

Buried beneath violets and daisies

Restless atop a poet's grave,

Rests in the earth mortal remains

Of an immortal name, for when inwrapt

In the hour of crepuscular embrace,

When the air of quiet death became

The taste of his breathless despair,

He welcomed his dying last breaths

By severing noctilucent threads

Of his lingering liminality,

Silver-spun by incorporeal light

When the Queen-Moon wept ecstasies

Upon Endymion's eternal sleep—

Before his living hand became cold

She poured spell-craft into her own:

An Orphean dream, a fragment of moon-stone,

A love-charm of white carnelian,

Now held within his hand of bone.

CLAY F. JOHNSON is an amateur pianist, devoted animal lover, and incorrigible reader of Gothic literature & Romantic-era poetry. His first collection of poetry, A Ride Through Faerie & Other Poems, *is forthcoming in 2021. Find out more on his website at www.clayfjohnson.com or follow him on Twitter @ClayFJohnson.*

17

Fertiliser
by Antonia Rachel Ward

Leaves crunch under your feet. The ground here is soft, layers slowly decaying. But beneath the soil, a network of roots reaches between the trees. They talk. They know it was you who harvested that willow for firewood. They felt the pain of your penknife slicing through an old oak's bark, carving your love's initials next to yours.

When that root trips you up, it's no coincidence.

Nor is the vine that wraps around your ankle. Nor the branch that drops suddenly, pinning you to the ground.

It takes energy to grow a network like this.

You'll make perfect fertiliser.

ANTONIA RACHEL WARD is a writer of horror, gothic and supernatural fiction based in Cambridgeshire, UK. Her short stories have been published by Black Hare Press and in the forthcoming COLP Underground *anthology by Gypsum Sound Tales. You can find her on Twitter @AntoniaRachelW1, Instagram @antoniarachelward or at antoniarachelward.com.*

18

Infertile Ground
by Michelle Mellon

I used to hate those "found object" stories. You know, the ones with some haunted item in an attic or cellar that lies waiting as an old house passes from owner to owner? Not my thing.

Until I became one.

It took four owners. Fifty years. Eighteen-thousand-two-hundred-sixty nights of pointless moaning and clacking. No one ever came down here. Not until the newest owner—the one with six kids—broke up the basement floor to finish the lower level.

I couldn't have kids. That's why I was down here, alone, where my murdering husband had buried my bones.

MICHELLE MELLON has been published in more than two dozen speculative fiction anthologies and magazines. She is a member of both the Horror Writers and Science Fiction and Fantasy Writers Associations. Her first story collection was published in 2018 and she's nearing completion on her second. For updates, visit www.mpmellon.com.

19

Gimme Shelter
by Petina Strohmer

Oh, I was ready.

My underground bunker contained enough food, water and fuel to last at least a year. People ridiculed doom-dayers, but we had the last laugh.

Eleven months have passed since the nuclear bomb dropped, or I assume it did - and there's nothing; on the radio or online. Have my devices died or is it everyone else? Is it safe to go outside and find out? How could I know?

My protected space has become my prison or, perhaps, my tomb.

Is it possible to die from loneliness? I have a horrible feeling I'm going to find out.

Originally from London, PETINA STROHMER now lives in Wales. Her first novel, Truly Blue; A Rock & Roll Parable, *was published by Leaf Books in March 2009. Her second novel,* Entertaining Angels, *was published by Cinnamon Press in May 2016. She also writes short stories, plays and magazine articles. For more information, go to petinastrohmer.com.*

20

What Comes After the Bombs?
by Joe Scipione

"Get underground," they said. "It's the only way to survive."

I listened. I stocked up on things needed to survive and went underground, avoiding the fallout of nuclear war. Three weeks later, I saw, heard, felt bombs go off. Through the window in my bunker, the world glowed green.

Time passed; weeks, months, years. My CB radio chirped.

"Hello," I said. "Anyone there?"

"Yes," a voice responded. "It's safe to come out."

"How can I be sure?"

"Just open the hatch," the voice barked.

I looked out the window, there were hundreds of them, but not a human among them.

JOE SCIPIONE lives in Illinois with his wife and two children. He is a senior contributor and horror book reviewer at horrorbound.net and a member of the Horror Writers Association. His debut novel Perhaps She Will Die *comes out in summer 2021. He can be found on Twitter or Instagram @JoeScipione0 and at joescipione.com.*

THE ROT BENEATH

21

Use Plenty of Organic Matter
by Dale Parnell

"I can manage fine."

"I don't want you overdoing it, Mum," Sarah fretted. "At least let Gavin give you a hand getting the potatoes in?"

The following Monday, Gavin arrived bright and early.

"I just want that bed digging over," Olive instructed firmly.

She returned a few hours later with a mug of tea, disturbed to see Gavin had dug up the rest of the vegetable plot.

"I thought I was helping," Gavin stuttered, unable to look away from the dozen skeletons buried in shallow graves.

"I wish you hadn't," Olive sighed, pulling an antique revolver from underneath her apron.

DALE PARNELL lives in Staffordshire, England, with his wife and their imaginary dog, Moriarty. He writes fiction, mainly fantasy, science-fiction and horror, along with the occasional poem. He has self-published two collections of short stories and a poetry collection to date, and is featured in a number of excellent anthologies. You can find Dale on Facebook at www.facebook.com/shortfictionauthor, and on Instagram at www.instagram.com/shortfictionauthor.

22

The Forgotten Do Not Forget
by Ryan B. Green

On the outskirts of Nervung lies a memorial long forgotten. No records remain of it nor visitors to pay their respects, save the vines that have reclaimed the stonework as their own.

One afternoon a swindler approached the town, aiming to pawn his concoction as the cure for all mortal ails. He beheld the memorial and—noting its glimmering form—resolved to investigate. In a flash the vines bound him, dragging his person beneath the ghastly foliage. As a final cruel act, they forced the bottle upon his lips, doing unto him what he had done to countless poor souls.

RYAN B. GREEN is a student at the University of Toronto studying Computer Science and Cognitive Science. With a lifelong love for reading, he is inspired by the works of masters such as H. P. Lovecraft and Edgar Allan Poe. For more information, visit ryanbgreen.ca.

23

Natural Causes
by Sean Reardon

I feel that my mother raised me well. She was single, but financially sound, so she expected things. She struck me with a whip until I was able to scrub from the rug any stains I made. She put her cigarettes out on my tongue when I lied. She poked me with her nail file when I didn't greet strangers with a smile. I grew to be a gentleman—clean, trusted, and charming. Just before I gutted her and let her intestines spill onto the carpet, she said, "This is beneath you, child." Cause of death was listed as "natural."

SEAN REARDON is a burgeoning short story author with a penchant for the macabre. He is currently pursuing a bachelor's degree in Creative Writing from Southern New Hampshire University and is a member of Sigma Tau Delta. Follow him on Twitter (@batpocalypse) for more from his dark digest!

24

House for Sale
by Lyndsey Croal

It was the furniture that stood out the most. In each room, it had been arranged against only three walls, as if part of a doll's house display.

"I suppose you'll want to see the basement too?" the owner offered.

There was a chill in the air as she led me downstairs. The house had been on the market for a year—maybe the basement had a damp problem. "How many viewings have you had?"

"You're the sixth." She switched the light on.

My breath caught. Beady eyes stared up at me, dolls sitting in a row. Five of them.

LYNDSEY CROAL is a Scottish writer based in Edinburgh. She received a Scottish Book Trust New Writers Award for 2020 and is working on her debut novel. Her work has been published in a number of anthologies, and her debut audio drama was recently produced by the Alternative Stories and Fake Realities *podcast. Find her on Twitter as @writerlynds or via www.lyndseycroal.co.uk.*

25

Hidden Cattleyas
by Umiyuri Katsuyama

Translated by Toshiya Kamei

I hook a rope ladder on the edge of the old well. Before his greenhouse went up in smoke during an air raid, my uncle hid his prized dark purple cattleyas at the bottom. Darkness engulfs me as I descend. My heart quickens. I'm so close to my uncle's cattleyas. How many times had I begged him to sell me some? He always answered, "They're yours when I'm dead." Ten steps later, I haven't reached the bottom. I look down. The abyss stares back. I drop a coin, but no sound follows. I search for the next step with my toes.

UMIYURI KATSUYAMA is a Japanese writer of fantasy and horror. In 2011, she won the Japan Fantasy Novel Award with her novel Sazanami no kuni. *Her latest novel,* Chuushi, ayashii nabe to tabi wo suru, *was published in 2018. Her short fiction has appeared in numerous horror anthologies in Japan.*

26

One World or None
by A. Whittenberg

Mama, how come you never told me about the A-bomb?

Were we too busy running from the men with pillowcases and sheets to duck and cover?

They claim we can't get a suntan, but are we also immune to gamma rays?

Is it like flesh coloured crayons, something that was created without us in mind?

There weren't whites only signs on the air raid shelters, so I guess they would have cracked open the door if we knocked hard enough, right?

We would have been one big, at last, happy family, at the end of the world, wouldn't we?

A. WHITTENBERG is a Philadelphia native who has a global perspective. If she wasn't an author she'd be a private detective or a jazz singer. She loves reading about history and true crime. Her other novels include Sweet Thang, Hollywood and Maine, Life is Fine, Tutored *and* The Sane Asylum.

27

Still of Dry Flowers
by Laura Keating

"Hold me, hold me close," she whispered.

"Of course, of course I will," she thought.

The cold of the night crept through the cracked iron door like a curious pet. Bolt cutters lay atop the decapitated lock.

"Hold me, hold me close," she whispered.

They had been denied a home together; here, then, was their humble abode. Secret and sparse. In the dark, they needed no furnishing. The thought was worth the risk, the laugh together.

"Hold me, hold me close," she whispered, smelling still of dry flowers and already of decay.

A kiss. "Of course, of course I will."

LAURA KEATING is a writer of thrillers, horror, and speculative fiction. Her work has been published in several anthologies, including Worst Laid Plans *from Grindhouse Press. You can follow her on Twitter at @LoreKeating, and find more of her work on her website, www.lorekeating.com.*

28

Cold Feet
by Caytlyn Brooke

The first one appeared on Sunday, just outside the church. Surrendering to the sun's stare, the ice block shortly unveiled the treasure encased within: a human hand.

More parcels of ice materialized.

A calf at the café, several toes at the school, and a torso at the grocery store. The victim was female, but her identity remained a mystery. Later that day, Detective Conner opened his door to find the smallest block yet. Beneath the glass-like surface, a phone rang. *Mom* flashed across the screen.

"Honey, Stacy isn't answering her phone," his wife called, as his stomach filled with dread.

CAYTLYN BROOKE is an award-winning author who enjoys creating horror stories from mundane rituals of daily life. With a degree in psychology, she studied fear and stimuli that make people uncomfortable. When she's not writing, she runs a daycare. She promises there are no children buried in the backyard. You can find her on Twitter @caytlyn_brooke or at https://www.bhcpress.com/Author_Caytlyn_Brooke.html

29

Asylum
by Claire Loader

"Come on now Margaret, it's time for mass."

I wondered how I was expected to pray, hands bound tight to the trolly, mouth gagged lest I scream. We do not rise to church but descend, the dark tunnel connecting ward and chapel damp with the stink of decay, paint peeling, lights flickering as the wheels of the trolly click their wary course.

"Now, you'll have to ask forgiveness this week won't we Margaret, hmm? For all that carry on?"

I lean my head to the side, eyes following the dusty pipes, knowing all too well: God does not visit hell.

CLAIRE LOADER is a New Zealand born writer now living in Galway, Ireland. Her dark fiction has appeared in various publications, including Harbinger Press, The Ginger Collect, Massacre Magazine *and* Dark Moon Digest.

30

Red Camellias
by Kirin Sasa

Translated by Toshiya Kamei

The white camellia tree in our garden bore red blooms one spring.

"It's a bad omen," I said, with a frown.

"Are you sure it bore white flowers before, honey?" My husband laughed and waved me off.

As the years went by, the red color of camellia blooms intensified. One day, I couldn't stand the sight any longer. I cut through the trunk. The tree toppled over. When I dug through the roots, human bones emerged.

"Oh no. You shouldn't have done that, honey." I heard my husband's voice behind me. When I turned, he flung down a blood-stained axe.

KIRIN SASA is a Japanese writer from Hyogo. Since 2016, she has published her fiction at Kakuyomu, *a Japanese site similar to* Wattpad. *In 2020, her short story was a finalist in the first Kaguya SF Contest.*

31

The Sinkhole
by David Fey

It started out small, as most things do.

A crack in the asphalt. A hole in the world.

By mid-afternoon a rust-bucket pickup groaned onto our street.

Its faceless driver dropped a quartet of orange safety cones around it.

By late evening the cones were gone, swallowed.

The mouth was growing.

Wider.

Hungrier.

Its acrid breath, moist and foul, bellowed over our lawns.

The neighbours' houses went dark.

The sky too. No moon. No stars.

No sound.

I crept out, phone-as-flashlight,

hand over face, eyes wet, throat scraped raw.

I stood at its edge.

I saw its teeth.

Its *teeth.*

DAVID FEY brings his fervent love of quiet horror with him to every expressive artistic corner he claws his way into. He's been a performing poet and singer/songwriter, a published photographer, and now works as an editor of young adult speculative fiction and horror for Angelella Editorial. You can find out more about David by visiting his website: ghostofdavid.com or following him on Twitter, @ghostofdavid.

32

A Beginner's Guide to Subtext
by Isaac Menuza

My husband hates a happy ending.

"A story is about subtext," he was fond of saying. "The emotions the film suggests, off-camera actions, words unspoken."

He loved to lecture me like this while I chopped vegetables for dinner, shoving cubed offshoots between his mealy lips. He would laugh and say I was silly for expecting resolution, for hoping that one godforsaken aspect of my life might be straightforward.

That I might at some point experience a climax.

Wink to the camera.

No such thing as happily ever after.

That's what he would say, anyway, if he still had a tongue.

ISAAC MENUZA is an author of speculative fiction and horror. He lives in Washington, D.C. with his wife, three children, and whatever slimy critters his son detains for temporary imprisonment. Find him on Twitter @Imenuza and at isaacmenuza.com.

33

Harvest Five
by Annabel Record

The first year the harvest wasn't right, we'd put it down to weather. Winter barely thawed into spring, a sodden summer followed. September, normally a month of crisp pink sunrises, turned so abysmal that some of the farmhands left.

"I've never seen anything rot so fast." One of the young men was thumbing potatoes that mulched in his fist. "There's no way we can ship these, Fin."

So I'd taken out loan after loan, eventually sold off the dairy.

One morning, the dogs came back crimson. And that's when we noticed. Blood, seeping up through the soil. Every single acre.

ANNABEL RECORD is a recent Master's graduate living in Central London. When she's not writing poetry or short stories, she can often be found running, reading, or dissecting politics over a pint.

34

It Is I
by Gabbie Frulla

You're trembling underneath your bed when it comes. You see its bare, bloody feet beside you. It knows you're there. The flames of your mother's religious candles on your nightstand flicker against the walls and stretch its shadow across them. Their light offers little hope because you don't believe in God, just luck.

The floorboards creek and it slowly crouches down to face you. You see a rabid version of yourself smiling back at you. You scream. *You* are the shadow creature that butchered your family in the middle of the night, and you will pay for your sins.

GABBIE FRULLA grew up next to a tiny cemetery in rural Connecticut where her love for horror blossomed. She travels through abandoned insane asylums in her spare time. She typically explores the themes of mental illness, sexual assault and feminine power in her writing. She encourages everyone to dip their feet into the horror pool because horror is healthy! You can find her on Twitter & Instagram: @ctgabbie.

35

9/11
by Austrian Spencer

My world has narrowed to this single detail, shaking, as I vibrate with our effort. I cannot breathe, cannot afford even that small luxury, as I stare at my hand, pumped crimson and rigid with her fear and hope, which I cannot maintain.

It is the end of my life.

I hear her muted sob as she realizes that we are done—that a life must end—that any life will never be long enough.

As my daughter's fingers slip, my scream breaks free. I stare into her eyes and into the nothing beneath her as she falls.

AUSTRIAN SPENCER is the author of The Sadeiest *from Darkstroke Books, and has a short story included in* Gothic Blue Book VI: A Krampus Carol *for Burial Day Books. He lives in Austria with his family under the forbearance of two cats who headbutt him for sport. You can find him at www.austrianspencer.com.*

36

Unmarked
by Jameson Grey

Beneath the damps of Yorkshire grey,

On craggy moors of untamed heath,

Two sisters stroll against the lay,

Wandering wilds to leave a wreath.

Long behind, the cobbled stone

That led them to this lonely place,

Its steepest climb—an act atoned—

The dreadful love they had to face.

Beyond scars of hatred shared,

Along, at last, with whispered grief,

Wuthering wind, ghosts of song bared,

While rainbow skies wrought rays in relief.

Their mother wronged—below the surface, known

Riven by rage to cleave this grave

Unmarked, their father, yet missed, was gone

And though unmarked, no-one was saved.

JAMESON GREY is originally from England but now lives with his family in western Canada. He also spent time in Asia as a child, which he understands makes him a fully-fledged third culture kid (TCK). His story "The Waiting Room" was published in The Toilet Zone: Number Two, *an anthology from Hellbound Books. He can be found online (occasionally) at jameson-grey.com and on Twitter @thejamesongrey.*

37

The Rot Beneath
by April Yates

A glossy veneer covers the rot that is us.

Beneath kind words uttered in public are ones reserved just for me.

Acidic and cutting.

The arm around my waist is my reminder that I shouldn't stray from them at parties; my place is by their side.

Beneath long t-shirts and jeans, is skin bruised and tender.

Kisses relented to for the camera are permission for them to take what they want at night, my consent irrelevant.

Beneath the mattress lays the knife, in case this is the night they go too far and I have to peel the veneer away.

*APRIL YATES lives in Derbyshire with her wife and some fluffy demons masquerading as dogs. A life long horror fan, she is subjecting herself to the horror of working simultaneously on both a novel and novella. Check out her website aprilyates.com for details about work forthcoming or find her lurking on Twitter @April_Yates_*

38

The Clog
by Mike Murphy

Joe kept moving the snake around in the clogged toilet. *Something* was in there. It wouldn't flush. He felt a sudden tugging—not the familiar sensation of breaking the clog, but of something on the other end!

Ez pulled and pulled. "It's coming!" he announced to the customer. Finally, he yanked the clog out. Disgusted, the woman looked away. Ez pulled the broken and bent form from the sonic toilet. Its shattered arms and legs hung loose at its side. He saw a patch on the garment it was wearing: "Joe's Plumbing."

Boy, he thought, *that* was *a deep clog.*

MIKE MURPHY has had over 150 audio plays produced in the U.S. and overseas. He's won The Columbine Award and a dozen Moondance International Film Festival awards in their TV pilot, audio play, short screenplay, and short story categories. His prose work has appeared in several magazines and anthologies. Mike is the writer of two short films, Dark Chocolate *and* Hotline. *In 2013, he won the inaugural Marion Thauer Brown Audio Drama Scriptwriting Competition. In 2020, he came in second. For several of the in-between years, he served as a judge. Mike keeps a blog at audioauthor.blogspot.com.*

39

The Killer in Me
by Stephen Howard

"Who are you?"

You want to know who is beneath the mask before they kill you. You lie there helpless, ankle broken.

The man's hand pulls at the flap beneath his chin and rolls back the skin-mask, an amalgamation of his previous victims. You freeze. Feel a tightness in your chest. It's… you.

A glint of sharpened steel, a star in the sky. But you stare only at your face. The killer's face. You know it worked. You perfected the time machine. But in travelling back, future you demented. Warped. Or was this always hiding within you?

The steel flashes.

STEPHEN HOWARD is a British novelist and short story writer with one novel and one short story collection to his name. Born and raised in Manchester, he now lives next to a graveyard in Cheshire with his partner, Rachel, and their demonic cat, Leo. His stories have been published by Lost Boys Press, Jazz House Publications, and others. You can find him on Twitter @SteJHoward and at www.stephenhowardblog.wordpress.com

40

Underneath the Overpass
by Paige Johnson

Sleepless in a shopping cart, the Wired Man writhes. He spits up frostbite-black syrup. Rat tongues spear at his spills, scavenge the scabs for protein as winter looms.

The Wire Man is cranked at the elbow, wound up by lithium and toluene. Fuse lit, he patrols the tunnel. Counts cars and graffiti etchings, protecting his fellow sludge-suckers. Lives locked inside a rusty soup can.

Faded off exhaust fumes, he staggers, all shark-toothed snarls and echoing rasps. "Pay the toll," he says on loop, rattling a coin cup.

Pedestrians call it, "Parkway psychosis."

He calls it "Home," then lights another match.

Like many strange stories, PAIGE JOHNSON hails from Florida. There, she runs a group called the Transgressive Mind, slated to publish its first "dirty realism" anthology in 2022. This comes alongside the release of her third novel, Where Me & the Vultures Live, *about an unlucky cam-girl.*

Fan Page: Facebook.com/ThePoliticiansDaughter

Fiction Group: Scribophile.com/groups/The-Transgressive-Mind/

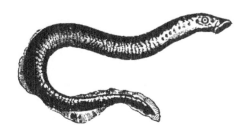

I'VE GOT YOU UNDER MY SKIN

41

Together
by Caitlin Marceau

The spade cracks the earth wide like an egg. He digs a perfect rectangle, then lowers the pine box into the ground. His wife had always hated his job, how he'd work through the night and come home smelling like dirt, with only pennies to show for his labour. Exhausted, he'd sleep through the day, and she grew lonely in his absence.

It's why she threatened to leave.

"Please," she sobs, scratching at the wood with bloody nails.

"It's what you wanted," he whispers back, "to spend more time together."

He fills in her grave, lantern flickering in the dark.

CAITLIN MARCEAU is an author and professional editor living and working in Montreal. She holds a B.A. in Creative Writing and is a member of the Horror Writers Association. If she's not covered in ink or wading through stacks of paper, you can find her ranting about issues in pop culture or nerding out over a good book. For more, check out CaitlinMarceau.ca.

42

Floaters
by Laura Nettles

The doctor called them floaters. The strange squiggles I would see dancing about my vision. Totally normal. Except mine formed into letters.

I was cleaning the bathroom when suddenly the letter "S" was drifting in front of the mirror. *Blink.* The curves changed. "O." *Blink.* "S."

I dropped the can of cleaner and blinked rapidly. "S," "O," "S." "S.O.S." The letters repeated in a frantic cycle, speeding up with the ferocity of my blinks. There was something trapped in my eye, beneath the surface. Behind the cornea and iris, deep inside my right eyeball. Something alive.

I plucked it out.

LAURA NETTLES is a California girl living in Canada. She lights creatures for horror films and enjoys penning her own tormenting tales. Follow her at lauranettles.com.

43

The Hunger Within
by Jeremiah Dylan Cook

My subject is secured to the autopsy table with his skin peeled back. I bend down and pull out the rib cage I've sawed free. I'm shocked by my discovery.

His heart is still pumping.

I've never made it this far with a person still alive. All my previous subjects perished when I opened them with my scalpel. It's a miracle.

I reach in and feel the organ beat.

When I look at the man's face, he smiles.

Pain jolts my arm. I yank out my hand and realize the skeleton beneath my flesh has been revealed to the world.

JEREMIAH DYLAN COOK is a horror writer who completed his master's degree in Writing Popular Fiction at Seton Hill University. He's a member of the Horror Writers Association and the managing editor of New Pulp Tales. You can learn more about him at www.jeremiahdylancook.com or follow him on Twitter @JeremiahCook1.

44

Body Text
by Robyn Pritzker

I was eleven when I started eating comic books, tearing off glossy fragments. Years later, I still consumed them every way I could, desperate to climb right inside.

Then, idly scratching at my arm last week, wide flakes began to come away like chipped paint. Looking down, I saw blue-black ink welling just below the skin. I peeled open my wrist and dug out a pulpy mass, uncrumpled it, saw panels, words, gutters—my own story.

More of me ripped apart. I unearthed stained pages from myself for days, until I felt an itching at my throat, the last chapter.

ROBYN PRITZKER is a lapsed antiquarian bookseller with a PhD in Gothic literature. She lives adjacent to a cemetery in Edinburgh, so she spends most of her time thinking about various hauntings. When she's not writing little weird things, she works as a learning technologist. You can find her on Twitter: @ robzker

45

Compulsion
by April Yates

It is both a beneficial and detrimental human trait, that compulsion you have to immediately touch or shove into your mouths anything new you find.

This is how you learned that the bright red berry is good; but not that other berry, oh no—that one will kill you.

How fortunate for me then, that having stumbled across me in my nice warm cave, the first thing you do is poke me, inviting me into your bloodstream like an old friend—and that you will then be so kind as to say to your companion.

"Hey, come check this out!"

*APRIL YATES lives in Derbyshire with her wife and some fluffy demons masquerading as dogs. A life long horror fan, she is subjecting herself to the horror of working simultaneously on both a novel and novella. Check out her website aprilyates.com for details about work forthcoming or find her lurking on Twitter @April_Yates_*

46

Upon the Wall
by Edward Brock

What is that upon the cave wall?

I do not know, I told them all.

Do please take a look, they ask of me.

I moved in close, not sure what I'd see.

As I looked upon the thing up there

It was strange and horrid, this I do swear.

Small like a fly, with sharp teeth and red eyes

It looked at me and the fear it did rise.

I turned, with alarm, but it leapt on my head.

Pierced my skin and filled me with dread.

Inside my brain, it did crawl

Telling me to kill them all.

EDWARD BROCK lives in a house, in a town, in between two mountains, in Virginia, with his wife and two dogs. He's published a handful of stories and articles, and is also a photographer. Find him on Instagram and Facebook as @edimaginer, or on Amazon: https://www.amazon.com/Edward-Brock/e/B005XMRECC?pldnSite=1.

47

Billy's Special Blanket
by Melody E. McIntyre

Billy tightened the blanket his mother made him around his head. She promised no monsters could hurt him through his special blanket.

The closet door creaked open and all of the monster's legs spilled out. It crawled across the floor and up onto the bed. A multitude of legs prodded Billy. The monster roared when it could not breach the blanket's power. In fury, the monster flailed about, destroying Billy's room.

His parents charged down the hall and through the door. Then screamed in terror when the creature attacked.

Billy was safe under the blanket, but his parents were not.

MELODY E. MCINTYRE lives in Ontario and has loved reading and writing her entire life. Her favourite genres to write are horror and mystery. She has published several short pieces of fiction. She studied Classics in University and remains obsessed with the ancient world to this day. You can find her on Twitter @evamarie41, Facebook @MelodyEMcIntyre and on her blog: melodyemcintyre.blogspot.com.

48

Skin Deep
by Keely O'Shaughnessy

My girlfriend, Kate, is an entomologist. Our flat is all cockroaches, maggots and fly larvae.

I show her the lump on my arm. Pinhead sized. Raised and red. The blackness at its centre could be teeth. She shrugs, dropping locusts into the mantis tank.

At night, something burrows beneath my skin. Leaching up, twisting.

"It could be a guinea worm," Kate teases.

As days pass, more lumps appear, causing ripples under my flesh; the teeth become gnashing jaws.

Confined to bed, I writhe as the welts pulse; my body no longer mine. Beside me, Kate waits, collectors jar in hand.

KEELY O'SHAUGHNESSY's stories have appeared online and in print. She has an MA from the University of Gloucestershire. She has writing forthcoming in the 2021 National Flash Fiction Day anthology and at Ellipsis Zine. *She is a Pushcart nominee. She's Managing Editor at Flash Fiction Magazine. When not writing, she likes discussing David Bowie with her cat. Find her on Twitter @KeelyO_writer.*

49

The Lovely Bones
by Fusako Ohki

Translated by Toshiya Kamei

"Could you take my place for a while?" a skeleton said, as her teeth rattled. "I want to get out and stretch my legs." She pointed her porcelain finger at a dirt pile next to an upturned grave. "You won't regret it."

I stepped into the pit and lay under a blanket of dirt. I waited and waited. While I waited, my flesh began to rot. My worries fell off with my skin. I chuckled as the worms tickled my ribcage. When she came back and dug me up, I too was a skeleton. Hand in hand, we frolicked together.

FUSAKO OHKI is a Japanese writer from Tokyo. She obtained her master's degree in Japanese literature from Hosei University. Her debut collection of short stories is forthcoming in 2021. Translated by Toshiya Kamei, Fusako's fiction has appeared in New World Writing.

50

A Strange Machine
by Benjamin Lawrence

The chrome contraption hummed with static in the corner of the basement.

"Ma'am... sorry, but there's no way your husband created a... *what* did you say? A *shrink ray?*" said the detective, spitting out a wad of gum, toeing a mass of fizzing wires with his shoe.

"That's the stuff of 10¢ comic books and Flash Gordon serials. Perhaps he ran away with his secretary? Happens all the time in suburbia."

He politely tapped his fedora and left the sobbing woman to fold her laundry, the screaming scientist disappearing up the stairs embedded in the gum beneath the detective's shoe.

BENJAMIN LAWRENCE lives in West London with his husband and French Bulldog 'Peggy', and he writes for shits 'n' giggles. He's had work published in a couple of horror anthologies now and loves the thrill of telling 'orrid stories to 'orrid readers. Ben's favourite food is cheese— it fuels the nightmares!

.

51

Scrabbling for Daylight
by Nicole M. Wolverton

The scratching started two days after I moved in. It was in the walls. Mice, maybe. Or raccoons. The frantic scrabbling of nails on wood grew louder by the day. I gouged holes in the walls, pried up floorboards. Nothing but a jagged scrape across my forearm to show for it. Blood oozed out of the cut, and the scratching noise intensified. I looked closer at my arm and shrieked when something wriggled, just beneath my skin. A long finger jutted out of the cut, then two. By the time a whole hand reached out, my screams froze to silence.

NICOLE M. WOLVERTON is a Philadelphia, PA fiction and nonfiction writer. Her short fiction has been previously published in magazines such as Aji *magazine,* The Molotov Cocktail, *and* Jersey Devil Press, *as well as in anthologies from Dark Ink Books, Haunted MTL, and Sliced Up Press, among others. She is also the author of* The Trajectory of Dreams *(Bitingduck Press, 2013). Find her online at www.nicolewolverton.com and @nicolewolverton (Twitter).*

52

What He Found in the Soil
by Isaac Menuza

Colin McGurty liked to sleep in graves.

Night after night, he set up camp in whatever new plot the diggers opened. Sleeping bag, pocket knife, and a cup of cafeteria pudding.

In the moon-glow, head on the turned earth, he said if he listened, the worms would speak to him.

"I got one with me," he said, holding up his hand.

A small purple hole bored into his palm, no telling how deep.

"They consume the living too." He tapped his forehead, muttering as he walked away.

Colin was a weird fucker.

But now I check my hands each morning.

ISAAC MENUZA is an author of speculative fiction and horror. He lives in Washington, D.C. with his wife, three children, and whatever slimy critters his son detains for temporary imprisonment. Find him on Twitter @Imenuza and at isaacmenuza.com.

53

I've Got You Under My Skin
by Tiffany Michelle Brown

You can't scream. I've gained control of your mouth, your breath, your throat. Your energy would be better spent enjoying these final moments. Soon, your flesh will be my flesh. This life of yours will have a new tenant. It's a difficult transition, I know, but it's easier if you don't fight.

Perhaps some memories will soothe you? Tomorrow will be a year to the day, you know. Our anniversary. You slipped into my lake, and I slipped into you.

Do you remember the warmth? The connection?

Hold onto that, sweet girl, because it's time for you to let go.

TIFFANY MICHELLE BROWN is a California-based writer who once had a conversation with a ghost over a pumpkin beer. Her fiction has been featured by Sliced Up Press, Cemetery Gates Media, Fright Girl Winter, and the NoSleep Podcast. You can find her on Twitter @tiffebrown or at tiffanymichellebrown.wordpress.com..

54

No Ordinary Headache
by Helen M. Merrick

"It's not a migraine. They're under my scalp, I can feel them moving."

"Tension headaches can cause the scalp to 'creep'. Are you stressed?"

"No."

"Taking medication?"

"No."

"I can prescribe painkillers."

"No! There's something in here." She tapped her skull hard. "They burrow into my brain, control me. Feel."

She grasped his hands, holding them on her head. Feeling movement, the doctor recoiled.

"Oh my…"

Wide-eyed, he watched a lump journey to her forehead. Blood spattered as it burst and a metallic spider-like creature emerged. It blinked red eyes, stretched its limbs, and leaped onto the startled doctor's face.

HELEN M. MERRICK lives in the UK Midlands with her family. When she's not teaching, she likes to scribble short stories and dream about writing a novel. She might, one day. You can find her at www.authorhelenmerrick.wordpress.com or on Twitter @HelenMerrick4.

55

If Ever
by Skye Pagon

I could feel it moving beneath my skin.

Slithering, skulking, sliding up my arm. *Wake up, you're dreaming,* some part of me cried. I wished I could believe it, but the proof was before my eyes: the undulation of the fascia of my forearm, the rippling of something beneath. How long would it take to reach some vital nerve, how long before I couldn't even think anymore? Oh God. If ever, reader, you feel that brush on the back of your neck, that hair raising sensation of *something* crawling across your skin, if ever that happens to you, you must—

SKYE PAGON is a New York based actor, writer, and theatre maker. You can find her written work at the Sword & Kettle Press, dramatics.org, and TheatreTrip.com, to name a few. She was a 2020 Best of the Net Anthology finalist for her poetry. @skyepagon on Instagram, www.skyepagon.com.

56

Skin Deep
by Ezekiel Kincaid

I slipped on the suit. The sleeves and pants still felt damp. Next time I'd have to let it dry for another hour, at least. I walked into the bathroom to check on Jim. He still lay in the bathtub moaning, with his skin removed and muscles glimmering in the flickering light. He slapped the side of the tub, leaving a bloody handprint. "Stop your complaining, Jim. Looks better on me than it did on you." I looked in the mirror and adjusted my new suit. I was never comfortable in my own skin, that's why I wore other people's.

EZEKIEL KINCAID has been published by Stitched Smile Publications, Grinning Skull Press, Lycan Valley Publications, Shacklebound Books, Horror Bites Magazine, Black Hare Press, Jakob's Horror Box, and Fantasia Divinity. His flash fiction story, "Deliquesce", won an honorable mention in the prestigious Dark Regions Press writing contest a few years ago. He also writes for Horror Bound *and* Puzzle Box Horror. *His first horror comedy novel,* The Adventures of Johnny Walker Ranger: Demon Slayer, *was released in February 2020 by Stitched Smile Publications. You can find him on Twitter @EzekielKincaid, Facebook @ezekethefreak or at https://ezekielkincaid.wordpress.com/*

57

They're in My Skin
by Alexis DuBon

Nobody believes me, because they can't see them. But that's because they know when to hide. They only come out at night. They squeeze themselves out from my tiny pores and go exploring across the plains of skin they've spent all day hiding under, grazing on my flesh when they think I'm asleep. But I can't sleep because I can feel them. I've taken baths in Clorox, I've really tried it all. And tonight, I'm going to light a fire. When my skin is all charred, they'll have nowhere to hide and everyone will see I'm not crazy. They're real.

ALEXIS DUBON spent most of her adult life waiting tables until quarantine, when, removed from all the real people out in the world, she decided to make up some new ones to keep her company. She lives in New York with her dog Schatzi. You can find her in Home *and* Cosmos, *anthologies of hundred word horror stories by Ghost Orchid Press and on Twitter @shakedubonbon.*

58

Beneath the Flesh, the Pain
by J.C. Robinson

The pain was becoming unbearable. Cramps, muscle aches, raw nerves.

She hadn't felt this awful ever before, and she couldn't comprehend what was causing it. Belle looked in the mirror at her ailing body and examined herself. She had gained weight.

Her eyes went large as she watched a ripple move beneath the stretched, tired skin of her stomach. Pain and fear like she had never before experienced shot through her system as she watched the skin of her stomach separate, the edges serrated and dripping with blood. She collapsed to the floor.

A rat scurried before her weeping eyes.

J.C. ROBINSON is a full-time law student, part-time writer. His debut novel, The Diner*, was published in March 2021, and he's currently working on a collection of short stories while preparing to take the bar exam. J.C. is a member of the LGBT community and loves reading horror from queer authors. You can find him on Twitter @jcr_scribe.*

59

Crawling
by Jessica Wilcox

The first time, it woke her from a deep sleep. She sat up, rubbing her arms until they stopped crawling. A nightmare, she told herself and fell back into a fitful sleep.

The second time was in the evening as she watched television. She swiped at her shoulder and looked for a spider, a bug, anything to explain what she felt.

The third time, she saw it. She sat at her desk at work when the skin on her leg raised and moved, something crawling beneath it. She screamed, cried, freaked out.

The fourth time, she had the knife ready.

JESSICA WILCOX (formerly Gilmartin) hails from Buffalo, New York, where she teaches English to refugees and immigrants. She resides with her husband, three children, two cats and puppy, all of whom keep her on her toes. You can find her on most social media platforms as @jawilcox711.

60

Even Your Death Can't Keep Us Apart
by Cara Mast

Greta hurries though the graveyard so the ringing of safety coffin bells at her passing might be mistaken for a breeze. She hopes he's ready this time. She's getting tired of these visits.

When she opens his casket lid, Julian stares silently at her, his face a freshly bloody ruin.

"Oh, love." She touches him and his wounds heal over. "Don't hurt yourself."

His tears wet her fingertips.

"So, you're not ready to come home with me?"

Julian continues to cry. Greta climbs out of the grave.

"See you next week, then."

He only quiets when she's buried him again.

As a retired tall-ship sailor, a failed academic, and a millennial finance professional, CARA MAST is someone who gets stopped constantly in New York City and asked for directions. Cara spends their free time drinking coffee, binging words, and yelling about the Philadelphia Eagles in their apartment and family group chat. They can be found on Twitter @digicara, and at digicara.com.

MALIGNANCY

61

Aftermath
by Emma K. Leadley

The avalanche quickly turned from a tragedy into a nightmare. Some kids had read the Cthulhu mythos and climbed the local mountain, at full moon, to summon an Old One. The snowy peak shook. Broadcast live from their phones, we watched those poor kids die.

Then, the ground split apart in random seams, spewing forth acid and fire. Countless lives were lost, and soon, humans were few. Our electronics were fried, the skies smoke-smothered. We lost our minds.

Stumbling round, we heard other survivors. Whispering assurance to them in the darkness, they trusted us. They shouldn't have: we were starving.

EMMA K. LEADLEY (she/they) is a UK-based writer, blogger and creative geek. She began writing as an outlet for her busy brain, and quickly realised scrawling words on a page is wired into her DNA. She's been published by multiple independent presses in the SFF and horror genres. Visit her on Twitter @autoerraticism or at https://www.autoerraticism.com/category/publications/

62

Death Gods Rising
by Hazel Ragaire

Survive. Survive beneath millennia of permafrost soil. In darkness we wait. Warmth's tendrils tease by degrees and our cage cracks. Long-dormant bacteria yawn embracing oxygen. We wiggle, yearning for hosts. Viral Sleeping Beauties will seek canvases for pain and pustules, painting pliable flesh with brilliant reds.

Above, we are extinct; no record of our conquests remain. We are death gods, coming. Life's and evolution's architects. We are not without mercy; you may prepare.

We will reap the land, bringing balance. My kin will burn or shrivel or suffer petri dishes. But some will sink back to darkness and thrive. Waiting.

Only ideas outnumber the horror books residing in HAZEL RAGAIRE's home. After years of teaching, Hazel decided to breathe life into words. When she's not conjuring up new characters or worlds, you'll likely find her plotting. Her favorite word is airneán, and you're welcome to join her anytime.

63

My Child
by Elford Alley

On Facebook, I show my child as I want her to be: smiles and bright eyes.

I preserve the thin veneer, the one eroding further every year. I mask the child whose presence makes animals howl, and who other children fear. I mask what's underneath, the fury that forces us to change schools and become nomads.

She grows impatient with me now. I cannot procure what she asks of me. I cannot hurt others. I don't understand the words she speaks, or how those words make a room cold and invite the unseen.

What happens when I cannot hide her?

ELFORD ALLEY is a horror writer. His stories have appeared in the Campfire Macabre *and* Paranormal Contact *anthologies. You can find his short story collections* Find Us, Ash and Bone, *and* The Last Night in the Damned House *on Amazon. He lives in Texas with his wife and children.*

64

Malignancy
by Evelyn Freeling

I'm what your mother warned you about years ago, smoke between your lips. You said there's a million ways to get me. You weren't wrong.

I'm in your blood now, globetrotting your organs, a parasite beneath your deceptively good health. You won't see me coming. Nobody does. I'll waste you until you can't recognize yourself in the hospital mirror. Until death looks like the kinder option. It is. Death's much kinder than I am.

I'll torment your children. For years, they'll wonder. They'll blame cigarettes, doctors, bacon, God. There's a million ways to get me. Later, I'll get them too.

EVELYN FREELING is a writer, mother and wife from the Pacific Northwest. She grew up in what she still insists was a haunted house. She harbours an obsession for things that give her nightmares and for turning nightmares into stories.

65

Swallow
by Erin M. Brady

He was so close to that rush of relief, he could almost taste it. He had come to realize that she was not kidding when she told him that she had a particular skill set. Hell, he was thankful to even be experiencing it.

What he didn't know was that she knew of his other violent and terrifying encounters with women like her. As she knelt below him, she thought of her sisters as his flesh began to tear. Soon his pants of pleasure turned into screams of agony, which were music to her ears as she swallowed him whole.

ERIN M. BRADY is a horror writer, film critic, and journalist based in Florida. She is currently an entertainment writer for Collider *and is working on numerous horror stories and screenplays. Her professional work can be read on erinmbrady.com, while her not-so-professional musings are relegated to her Twitter @erinmartina.*

66

Resident of the Box
by J.J. Kīmmorist

The box bumps along in the passenger seat of your car. You try to keep your eyes up, but you keep glancing over at it. The latch is closed tight, but you feel an itch under your collar. Sweat percolates your brow.

Far into the outback, you pull over. Lighter fluid. A small fire will do.

You open your passenger side door. Before you burn it, you want one last look beneath the lid. You can't help it. Your hands tremble as you undo the clasp and tilt open the lid to peer inside.

It's empty.

Shit. You fucked up.

J.J. KĪMMORIST is a fantasy/science-fiction/horror author from Nashville, Tennessee. She is a metalhead and avid horror movie connoisseur and enjoys anything to do with the macabre. She lives with her husband, sister, nephew, and two spindly greyhounds in a creepy house on a hill. You can find J.J. at www.kimmorist.com.

67

Half-Life
by Laurence Sullivan

Max first felt something was wrong when the flowers lost their fragrance. Their aroma had accompanied him throughout the construction of his cabin, but now the whole forest seemed to lack its signature scent.

Soon after, bruises started spreading across his body like ink blots—staining his thinning skin a sickly shade of puce.

By the time the bleeding began... it was already far too late.

Max could never have known the cause of his sickness had been radiating out from beneath his feet.

Undocumented nuclear waste.

It would be years before somebody finally found him.

But not nearly long enough…

Runner-up in the Wicked Young Writer Awards: Gregory Maguire Award, LAURENCE SULLIVAN'S creative writing has appeared in such places as: Londonist, The List, NHK World-Japan, Literary Orphans *and* Popshot Quarterly. *He became inspired to start writing during his studies at the universities of Kent, Utrecht, Birmingham and Northumbria—after being saturated in all forms of literature from across the globe and enjoying every moment of it. More of his work can be found online at www.laurencesullivan.co.uk and on Twitter @LozzySullivan*

68

The Fluffer
by Katie Young

Pol set down her carbide lamp and resumed scraping. A greasy concoction of metal filings, brake dust, and human detritus—sucked into the inky tunnels by trains—clung to the rails.

"Polly put the kettle on..." Hushed sing-song voices again.

"Edith? Peggy? Leave off!" But Pol *knew* it wasn't her workmates' japery.

She shuddered. A mouse scampered over her foot. Another. More. The darkness alive with scurrying creatures.

She snatched up the lamp. Not mice.

Teeming clumps of oily lint, teeth, hair. Dried blood. Ground bone. Memories. Myriad whispers.

Pol stumbled. Her ankle snapped, and her screams joined the cacophony.

KATIE YOUNG is a writer of dark fiction. Her work appears in various anthologies including collections by Nyx Publishing and Fox Spirit Books, and her story, "Lavender Tea", was selected by Zoe Gilbert for inclusion in the Mechanic Institute Review's Summer Folk Festival 2019. She lives in North West London with her partner, an angry cat, and too many books. You can find her on Twitter @pinkwood.

69

Interview Room One
by Dale Parnell

"Where is she, Robbie?"

"Robert," I correct him.

"Where is she, *Robert*?" he repeats.

I can tell he doesn't like me. I've been sitting here for hours, staring at that mirrored wall.

"He took her under," I whisper, for the hundredth time.

"Under where, Robert?"

Under the house, I want to tell them, down through the solid floor without leaving a single mark. But how can I? They'll think I'm crazy, that I hurt her. How do you explain that your girlfriend has been taken by something that didn't look quite human? Something wrong and twisted. Something wearing your face.

DALE PARNELL lives in Staffordshire, England, with his wife and their imaginary dog, Moriarty. He writes fiction, mainly fantasy, science-fiction and horror, along with the occasional poem. He has self-published two collections of short stories and a poetry collection to date, and is featured in a number of excellent anthologies. You can find Dale on Facebook at www.facebook.com/shortfictionauthor, and on Instagram at www.instagram.com/shortfictionauthor.

70

The Things You'll Miss
by Vivian Kasley

You've no idea how much you'll miss some things until you do. But the one thing I miss more than absolutely anything is looking up at the stars. We used to do it on clear nights, especially clear summer nights, when the air was as sticky as the raspberry popsicles in our hands and the fireflies flickered around us in droves. I wish I hadn't squandered my time so much on pointless stuff, but I never thought we'd be underground, hidden away from the world like living time capsules. Mostly, down here, we just painfully long and long and long...

VIVIAN KASLEY hails from the land of the strange and unusual, Florida! She's a writer of short stories which have appeared in various science fiction anthologies, horror anthologies, horror magazines, and webzines. Her street cred includes Blood Bound Books, Dark Moon Digest, Gypsum Sound Tales, HellBound Books, Castrum Press, and Sirens Call Publications. She's got more in the works, including an upcoming tale in Vastarien *and her very first novella.*

71

Brood X
by Sheri White

In 2004 the 17-year cicadas emerged in the Mid-Atlantic as expected. Just a noisy nuisance, harmless. But while waiting to burrow out of the dirt, they evolved from harmless herbivores to ravenous carnivores.

Sharp teeth and a thirst for warm blood compelled them to attack. Swarms covered people and animals, ripping flesh from bone. Millions watched YouTube videos, shot by horrified onlookers through windows and door cracks. The cacophony of victims' screams and cicada mating songs was unbearable.

This year, scientists saturated the earth with chemicals to keep them underground.

It didn't work.

They're here and dear God, they're *hungry*.

SHERI WHITE lives in Maryland with her husband Chris, as well as one of their daughters, her five-year-old granddaughter, one dog, and four cats. Life is not dull even with a quarantine! Her stories have been published in many anthologies and magazines. Find her at: https://www.facebook.com/sheriw1965/ or on Twitter @sheriw1965.

72

The Root of All Evil
by Andrew McDonald

Paul pulled himself from the wreckage. Sirens grew louder. Ignoring his injuries as best he could, he pulled the bag of money from under the passenger's seat where it was wedged.

He ran into the thick woods. Adrenaline was wearing off, and the slug in his side ached.

His lungs burned, his legs screamed, he leaned against an old tree for a moment. Paul noticed a hole under the tree that looked big enough to hide in. Crawling under the tree, he waited.

Roots erupted from the dirt, constricting him. Digging into his wound, the tree started to drink.

ANDREW MCDONALD lives in St. John's, Newfoundland and Labrador, Canada with his wife and daughter. His short story "First Visit" was included in Pulp Science Fiction from The Rock by Engen Books.

73

Fracking
by Julie Sevens

Earthquakes shouldn't happen in Oklahoma, but the ground rumbles under Kristi's feet. The earth shatters, a dinner plate scattered on the kitchen floor. The brand new hydraulic drills collapse into the earth's fiery innards. Hot steam bursts from new scars.

Smoky shadows crawl on their bellies across floating islands of dirt and field. The shadows drag towards her white-washed farmhouse, dry dust whirling behind them.

Their edges distend as they gorge on the fuel in her propane tank and her pickup. From a cold, dark upstairs window, Kristi watches them ooze back into the cracks, reclaiming what she had taken.

JULIE SEVENS is an Ohioan who transplanted to Philadelphia and Berlin before settling in the Chicago area with her family. You can find more of her nightmares at juliesevens.com.

74

Vampire Kiss
by Matthew Barron

Handsome Count Renaud made love to Mae the first time that night.

"The castle is yours while I sleep, but never enter the crypt below."

Mae's lantern lit twisting stairs. Within the coffin, a bloated stomach bulged though Renaud's faded coat, while the rest of the body within was a dry mummy.

Thick lips curled into a cup lined with concentric rows of teeth. "You can't unsee what you have seen."

"I don't want it to end." She leaned toward the pulsating lips, but she couldn't force herself to kiss him.

Mae returned to her father's house the next morning.

MATTHEW BARRON spends his days mixing and analyzing human blood as a medical technologist in Indianapolis Indiana. Matthew's short stories have appeared in Outposts of Beyond, Sci Phi Journal, Ill-Considered Expeditions, Roboterotica, House of Horror, *and more. He's also released three graphic novels and produced two short plays for the Indianapolis Fringe festival. His latest book is a paranormal mystery called* Buried Curses. *For more information, visit http://www.submatterpress.com*

75

Her Parting Gift
by Anna Sanderson

Susie left nothing behind but a crudely drawn map. Another game! Still, curiosity soon got the better of me, and I followed her scribbles to an abandoned field where frantic fingers clawed at the earth, taking my break-up frustrations out on the damp soil until I reached Susie's surprise. There, beneath the ground, the last in a long, neat line, was my heart. Badly bruised, but still beating. So that's where she'd been hiding it! I reached down, gently scooping it up into my bloodied palm. I had no use for it anymore, but Susie didn't need to know that.

ANNA SANDERSON is a writer from Nottingham, England, who writes about the world as she sees it (with the odd twist and turn). Her work can be found online at sites like 101 Words and Fifty Word Stories, and in numerous zines and anthologies. Find her on Twitter at @annasanderson86.

76

Beneath Her Skin
by Toshiya Kamei

"Honey…" I frown as Masami sheds another layer of her skin. Each time, she becomes slightly smaller. She reminds me of my grandmother's matryoshka dolls.

"Does it hurt?" I ask. She shakes her head no.

I pick her skin off the floor and hold it against the daylight. The translucent, flimsy coat retains her impression. It's like a shed snakeskin lying over a low shrub.

"I'll have nothing of you left," I mumble.

"But you'll have my skin."

The finality of her life hits me, and I swallow tears. Masami flashes a thin smile and hugs me.

TOSHIYA KAMEI is a fiction writer whose short stories have appeared in New World Writing, Trembling With Fear, *and* Utopia Science Fiction, *among others.*

77

Screaming Darkness
by Laura Nettles

Disinterred dust billows around my sneakers. The Paris catacombs confine me, squeezing me onward through their narrow tunnels. Hallways of water fill my shoes. The graffiti stopped miles back.

Something screams behind me.

I whip around, my hair raising at the dark emptiness lined in looming, shadowy bones.

Jogging, I try to remember the directions to the nearest manhole exit to the surface. My phone died hours ago, so I'm going on memory. The flashlight flickers. A shriek sounds directly behind my right ear, something swiping at my blistered feet. I drop the flashlight and sprint. Screaming darkness consumes me.

LAURA NETTLES is a California girl living in Canada. She lights creatures for horror films and enjoys penning her own tormenting tales. Follow her at lauranettles.com.

78

Sigils & Whispers
by Micah Castle

Disease deadened me from the collar down; no cure to be found. You said you knew a way to fix me; and without options, I agreed. Lying on the floor, I counted ceiling tiles.

Your hands parted my belly like the sea, and if I could, I'd feel your blood-slick fingers delicately scribble sigils on my insides; your warm breath whispering gibberish into me; the cold metal needle stitching me closed.

You sat up, held your breath…

Tingling coolness erupted beneath once numb flesh. You pressed your palm to the sutures; I felt your hand there for the first time.

MICAH CASTLE is a weird fiction and horror writer. His stories have appeared in various places, and he has three collections currently out. He enjoys spending time with his wife, aimlessly hiking through the woods, playing with his animals, and can be found reading a book somewhere in his Pennsylvania home. You can find him on Twitter @micah_castle, Reddit r/MicahCastle, and on micahcastle.com.

79

New Light
by Gus Wood

We're deep enough to go blind now.

Roger, Hannah, Mitchell, and me.

We have to rely on smell, sounds, and touch to get a hold of what our flashlights fail to find.

I'm at the back. The Anchor. Making sure no one gets lost.

The pain in my ankle is getting worse.

The bite from earlier keeps rubbing against its bandage.

It's dark. Getting darker.

The fever's getting worse. I'm sweating. My teeth ache with new growth.

I turn off my flashlight. I don't need it anymore. I can see everything.

Even the three intruders.

Fumbling around.

In my cave.

GUS WOOD is a game designer who writes about horror movies. You can find his work at https://gusfuss.itch.io/ (Games) and https://gusonhorror.myportfolio.com/ (movie writing). He hopes you read this by candlelight.

80

Fridge in the Basement
by Aaron E. Lee

A grey mutation has grown out from under the lids and curdles in shallow divots. A pungent draft swims through your nostrils... you won't ever forget again. The cold wet bowels weren't sealed. The dank dim room lit by a single flickering bulb hides a hideous truth. The casserole wouldn't have lasted one week—you gave it four. The phlegm of noodles starts to wriggle and squirm. You swing the refrigerator door closed and though you've headed back up the stairs, you hear a *eek eek* and scratching as the fleshy mass is eaten by your most unwanted house guest.

AARON E. LEE graduated from the University of Oklahoma in 2006. He has published 3 collections of short stories that can be found on Amazon.com. His newest short story "Heatwave" appears in the anthology Remnants *created by Stephen Coghlan.*

IT LURKS BELOW

81

Guided Meditation
by Kati Lokadottir

We laid on our yoga mats, exhausted after the session, and the new instructor started the guided meditation.

"Imagine a beautiful field in the warm, afternoon sun. Butterflies frolic in a gentle breeze that embraces you with the fragrance of bluebells. You feel safe and joyful. Take a deep breath and slowly let it out. In, and out. The ground shakes gently and opens at your feet. A demon climbs out of the hole and offers you his hand. Take it."

He watched as we were pulled out of our bodies, demons dragging us into Hell as their joyful slaves.

KATI LOKADOTTIR is your weird girl next door. She reads tarot, writes posthumous fiction and learns throat singing inspired by The Hu. Keep an eye out for her as she shares her writing with the world on Facebook and Twitter - just search her name! And why not write her something nice at katilokadottir@gmail.com?

82

Blood Ahoy
by Dee Grimes

The ocean floor yawns wide

when hunger pulls her from its depths.

She dines at night

vessels tickling her tonsils,

passengers wail in agony

as they burn in her belly—

bows of ships are wedged in her molars.

Whales are mere minnows

as they slide along her tongue

and into an abyss of bubbling bile.

Red flows into dark blue,

and the waters churn purple

against her black, crusty skin,

as her reptilian mass glides, and dives.

Long, has she hunted in the briny deep

but her affinity for seafood has waned;

eyes of slate are surveying the shore.

DEE GRIMES is a poet and fiction writer from St. Michael, Barbados. She has won NIFCA awards for her poetry and essay writing and her work has been featured in ArtsEtc Winning Words *anthologies. Dee is currently writing her first collection of dark poems and short stories. You can find her on Twitter @DHGrimesbb*

83

Lake of Fire
by Julia Ross

Far below the first crust of the earth, beyond the soil and worms, is a lake of fire that's too dark to be described as black.

We don't have much choice but to cross the lake upon our arrival, provided we've brought sufficient payment. The truly lucky ones are those buried without coins in their coats, for resurfacing would surely be much easier without having flesh and bone melt during attempts to swim against the flames.

We're told fighting against the boiling waves is impossible, that once you cross the dark lake, you're here for eternity.

But still, we try.

JULIA ROSS is a horror writer based in Phoenix, Arizona. Though reading and writing are among her favorite activities, she spends most of her time looking at the suspicious pile of clothes on her chair that appears to have a face. You can find her on Twitter @__jr0__

84

It Lurks Below
by Lilly Tupa

Far down beneath the darkest depths
You will hear a heavy rasping breath
One that strikes the deepest fears
And causes all joy to disappear

You wish not to see the ever smiling face
The one that they have deemed disgraced
It lurks and hides below the rock
Deep below your shoes and socks

But if you happen to catch a glimpse
Don't let the teeth and eyes eclipse
The fear that you should feel within
That crawls right through your bones and skin

It will gladly tear you limb from limb
Then take the place of where you've been.

LILLY TUPA is a young aspiring writer. She spends most of her time creating, whether that be through words or textiles and fabrics. She tends to read more than write to her own chagrin and dreams of one day being the creator of others' fictional heroes. Though she has only a few published pieces writing continues to be her passion.

85

The Dreamer
by Kristin Cleaveland

It is darker than midnight—desolate and cold. Strange creatures, prickling with venom, drift and float in the bitter brine, spreading stinging arms in a warning.

Dim, bulbous eyes cast around, almost blind, for the darting movements of weaker prey. No light but the faint, phosphorescent glow of monsters nearly as old as time itself.

At the lowest point, where no other can descend, he rests. Blood shot through with salt pumps through ancient veins. Through every age of man, he has slumbered; his time has not yet come. In a valley impossibly deep, he sleeps. He dreams. He waits.

KRISTIN CLEAVELAND writes horror and dark fiction. Her debut short story, "Lilith, My Daughter", appeared in the Winter 2021 issue of Black Telephone Magazine. *She has a master's degree in English and has worked as a writer, editor, proofreader, and educator. Find her on Twitter as @KristinCleaves.*

86

The Graveyard
by Nerisha Kemraj

Anthropological teams arrived on site to find hundreds of gigantic bones wedged within the sediment.

"Be careful not to damage anything. This could very well be the largest discovery of giants known to man."

The team set to work, uncovering bones, drilling, busting rocks—careful not to disrupt the natural flow of the cave.

Three hours into extraction, the ground began to shake when heavy thuds, followed by growls, resounded throughout the cave.

Torchlight revealed human-like eyes full of rage, each the size of a basketball, staring back, while enormous hands reached out, ripping heads off from each human they grabbed.

The exits were blocked.

NERISHA KEMRAJ resides in Durban, South Africa with her husband and two mischievous daughters. While poetry has been a love since high school, she began writing short stories in 2016. A lover of dark fiction, she has over 180 short stories and poems published in various publications, both print and online. She has also received an Honourable Mention Award for her tanka in the Fujisan Taisho 2019 Tanka Contest.

Nerisha holds a Bachelor's degree in Communication Science, and a Post Graduate Certificate in Education from University of South Africa. You can find her on Facebook @Nerishakemrajwriter or on Amazon: https://www.amazon.com/author/nerisha_kemraj

87

Ripples
by Carys Crossen

The dairy was built above a sluggish river. The eels came to drink the milk spilled into the water.

A city grew around and over the river. The waters mouldered in Stygian dark, but the eels still visited where the dairy had been. It was tradition.

One eel decided to remain there always. It liked the safe cool dark. And there were plenty of human leavings to eat.

It grew. And grew. So did its hunger.

It grew so enormous that the buildings above trembled when it moved.

A maintenance worker was the first to vanish. But not the last.

CARYS CROSSEN has been writing stories since she was nine years old and shows no signs of stopping. Her fiction has appeared online and print, and her monograph "The Nature of the Beast" is available from University of Wales Press. She lives in Manchester UK with her husband and their beautiful, contrary cat. You can find her on Twitter @AcademicWannabe.

88

Canary Red
by Josh Sippie

We stopped naming the canaries. After Midge, Milo, Beauregard, Thurgood, Winston, and Violet all disappeared less than a day into their sacred duties, it became a pointless use of mental fortitude. We'd heard of canaries dying in the mines—that was kind of the point—but they weren't dying. They were disappearing. Or they *had* disappeared, rather. Past tense, since I could see them now in the lantern light, prancing around the gristly remains of the foremen, covered in vibrant red offset by their natural sunshine yellow feathers. Their soulless black pebble eyes found mine just before their beaks did.

JOSH SIPPIE lives in New York City, where he's the Director of Publishing Guidance at Gotham Writers. His writing can be found or is forthcoming at McSweeney's Internet Tendency, The Writer Magazine, Brevity, Sledgehammer Lit, Wretched Creations, *and more. He has ongoing columns at* Hobart, Points in Case, *and* Daily Drunk Mag. *More at joshsippie.com or @sippenator101.*

89

Unique Selling Point
by April Yates

The cave comes with the house, a unique selling point. You don't even have to go outside to access it—the whole house is structured around it. There's even a handy staircase for you to descend into its depths on.

What lurked beneath had long lost use of her eyes; muscles grown atrophied from disuse.

She'll look after you, though.

That promotion you want, yours. That person who once bullied you, vanished with nothing to tie you to it.

There is one thing that she wants for herself, but her womb has shrivelled and wasted.

She'd like to borrow yours.

*APRIL YATES lives in Derbyshire with her wife and some fluffy demons masquerading as dogs. A life-long horror fan, she is subjecting herself to the horror of working simultaneously on both a novel and novella. Check out her website aprilyates.com for details about work forthcoming or find her lurking on Twitter @April_Yates_*

90

Skritch
by R.J. Joseph

SKRITCH.

Me and Sissy startled.

"Wood rats beneath the floor. Eat," Mama said.

We ate our daily rice with watery gravy.

Mama stayed hungry.

SKRITCH. SKRITCH.

They stayed hungry.

Mama cussed the landlord because he said he ain't seen no rats.

She smiled at the man at the corner store and got some poison.

She patted the lumpy stick she kept near our bed in case Daddy broke in again.

SKRITCH. SKRITCH.

We ain't have to worry about him no more, but she didn't know that.

They got him.

They ain't no rats.

They ain't staying down there forever.

R.J. JOSEPH earned her MFA in Writing Popular Fiction from Seton Hill University and lives in the suburbs of Houston. She has had stories and essays published in various venues, including three Stoker Award™ finalists. Her essay, "The Beloved Haunting of Hill House: An Examination of Monstrous Motherhood", is also a Stoker Award™ finalist for 2020. You can often find her "not writing" on Twitter @rjacksonjoseph.

91

Demontia
by Kevin Skirrow

The doctors say it's Alzheimer's, I know better. The professionals tell my family that I'm losing my memories; that part they've nearly got right. I'm not losing them; they're slowly being devoured.

I've tried to tell them, shouted until I'm hoarse, but all they do is medicate me. It's for my own good they tell me.

Lights out.

I can hear it crawling out from beneath my bed. I try to fight the effects of the drugs but my body, my voice, won't respond.

Its hand reaches for me.

Why does it leave the memory of itself?

Let me forget.

KEVIN SKIRROW was born in Shropshire, England, in 1981. He used to live in Transylvania and is an aspiring horror writer. Demontia was the first story he ever wrote, and he hopes you enjoy it.

92

Under the Ice
by Melody E. McIntyre

I came to the lake to rescue my sister. Ice covers its surface and I drop to my knees. Together, we bang against the icy barrier between us as I spout useless apologies. Her angry eyes gut me. I didn't mean to condemn her to this when I brought her body here. Local legend claimed she would come back on the thirteenth day of winter. It did not mention the ice.

With a loud crack, her hands break through.

Joy fills me but quickly turns to terror when instead of escaping, she pulls me down under the ice with her.

MELODY E. MCINTYRE lives in Ontario and has loved reading and writing her entire life. Her favourite genres to write are horror and mystery. She has published several short pieces of fiction. She studied Classics in University and remains obsessed with the ancient world to this day. You can find her on Twitter @evamarie41, Facebook @MelodyEMcIntyre and on her blog: melodyemcintyre.blogspot.com.

93

Johnny's Last Surf
by Alexis DuBon

Just below the surface, only barely out of reach,

Johnny left her body buried in the sandy beach.

Her soul escaped that shallow grave, abandoned in the dark;

And swept up by the tide, she found her way inside a shark.

In the depths she waited, under waves and salty cover,

For the moment she would have revenge upon her lover.

Patiently she waited, knowing when he did return,

He'd then understand the pain of retribution's burn.

The last thing that he felt before he filled the sea with red,

Was terror only vengeance knows, the deepest kind of dread.

ALEXIS DUBON spent most of her adult life waiting tables until quarantine, when, removed from all the real people out in the world, she decided to make up some new ones to keep her company. She lives in New York with her dog Schatzi. You can find her in Home *and* Cosmos, *anthologies of hundred word horror stories by Ghost Orchid Press and on Twitter @shakedubonbon.*

94

Never Alone in Hallowed Ground
by Brianna Malotke

The marble entrance
Of the mausoleum was almost
Welcoming in appearance.
Inside, the air was damp,
Stone walls cold to the touch,
The silence intensifying
With every passing moment
Spent enclosed.
She made her way
Down the stone steps
—deeper and deeper—she went
Beneath the earth,
Well below the six feet
Others around her were laid
To rest for eternity.
In this hallowed ground,
roaming the pitch black tunnel,
Searching for the right exit.
Every heartbeat thumping loudly
Against her chest.
There was an echo, slightly offbeat,
It was then, in between beats,
She realized she was not alone.

BRIANNA MALOTKE is a freelance costume designer and writer based in Illinois. Her most recent publications include a feature of three horror poems on The Yard: Crime Blog *in December 2020. Looking ahead, in 2022 she will be a Writer in Residence at the Chateau d'Orquevaux in Orquevaux, France.*

95

Fathom
by Eilidh Spence

It's been dark since I hit 200 metres.

The radar's doing most of the heavy lifting, of course. Still, it's harder without being able to see outside of this utterly minuscule submarine.

I hear a ping. Something's there.

I try to look; through the window, I can almost see something. It's close to the lamp, then.

I see a huge, black circle ringed in milky white, set in a vast pale mass. Warped and twisted red tendrils branch out from its centre like distorted lightning; its edge is pockmarked with wiry white fibres, coarse and sick.

And slowly, it blinks.

EILIDH SPENCE lives in Scotland with her parents and sibling, but more importantly, with their three cats. When not writing, she enjoys designing and sewing her own clothes and listening to a variety of podcasts. When forced, she will spend some time studying her ongoing Computing Science degree.

96

The Fish Have Eaten Her Eyes
by Nicola Kapron

My sister sleeps beneath the waves. Around her, the sea smells of rot and old blood. The fish have eaten her eyes; her skin sloughs off in strips, mingling with seafoam. I keep my boat well out of her reach when I come to check on her. There was a time when she held me close and swore she would never hurt me. Then our village sacrificed her. Promises mean nothing now.

Her face is a grinning skull. The chain around her ankles has almost rusted through.

I wonder what it's like to drown. I suppose I'll know soon enough.

NICOLA KAPRON has previously been published by Neo-opsis Science Fiction Magazine, *Nocturnal Sirens Publishing, Rebel Mountain Press, Soteira Press,* All Worlds Wayfarer, *and Mannison Press. Nicola lives in Nanaimo, British Columbia, with a hoard of books—mostly fantasy and horror—and an extremely fluffy cat.*

97

The Echoes
by Georgia Cook

She heard them sometimes, down in the deeper tunnels: not voices, as some of her fellow cavers claimed. Not footsteps or whispers.

She tried to explain, but could only find the words when she was already down below, sliding through the gaps beneath the earth.

The cave network was punishingly cramped, leading on and on through tight dark passages and jagged corridors, opening suddenly into vast black caverns before contracting again.

Like a gullet.

Like the mouth of a beast.

And through them all, echoing even in the deepest silence, calling her on ever downward: that muffled boom. That heartbeat.

GEORGIA COOK is an illustrator and writer from London, specialising in folklore and ghost stories. She is the winner of the LISP 2020 Flash Fiction Prize, and has been shortlisted for the Bridport Prize, Staunch Book Prize and Reflex Fiction Award, among others. She can be found on twitter at @georgiacooked and on her website at https://www.georgiacookwriter.com/

98

Log Entry #0156
by Sophie Sadler

Veryovkina Cave. Depth: 2,212 metres. My team and I have been down there for a week, charting the deepest passages on Earth. Only a few hours ago, we discovered a new tunnel.

I entered first, leaving my colleagues behind. Moments passed; their voices faded.

Then, light. I emerged, impossibly, on the grass by the limestone rocks surrounding the cave entrance. My depth now: 0 metres. Worse, I am alone. The tents, here ten days ago, are missing. My teammates, apparently gone.

Protocol F5: Never leave your crew. Protocol S12: Retrace steps when necessary.

I crawl to the cave mouth edge.

SOPHIE SADLER is a PhD candidate living in Wales where she spends her time hiking, riding her horse Bounce, and writing for fun. You can find her at sophiesadler.com.

99

Ready for Drowning
by Claire Hunter

A reservoir now, Llyn Celyn sits still and dark with the depth of her secrets. Underneath the surface lie the bones of a village sacrificed; twelve homes drowned, walls coated with the slime of river-reeds and greed.

The road to the lake chokes with abandoned cars. Their owners, tourists, ensnared by the moonlit glitter on the water. Car doors are left open, engines running; eventually they will be towed but more will come.

Below opaque waves the village screams for vengeance. A beauty spot with a feral darkness beneath; guests suffocate in the depths.

The view is to die for.

CLAIRE HUNTER currently lives in Liverpool. She enjoys writing dark fantasy and has won a writing contest hosted by the University of Liverpool, where she is studying for her Masters in Nursing. She is an active member of the writing site Scribophile. This is her first publication.

100

The Pit
by Patrick Winters

He'd been worshipped once. Revered by a people who rejected the False God of the heavens, knowing that true might rested within the earth. His might, his earth. They would offer up herds of themselves as sacrifice, summoning him from below with the raucous pounding of their drums and the wailing of their voices.

He stirred now, hearing a similar call, and climbed through the darkness to answer.

As he burst from the ground, the people above scattered, fleeing in terror.

Confused, he looked down to a great platform at his feet. The banner across its pillars read: "MetalFest 2021"

PATRICK WINTERS is a graduate of Illinois College in Jacksonville, IL, where he earned a degree in English Literature and Creative Writing. His work has been featured throughout several magazines and anthologies. A full list of his previous publications may be found at his author's site:
http://wintersauthor.azurewebsites.net/Publications/List

ACKNOWLEDGEMENTS

I was delighted and amazed by the success of our first Hundred Word Horror anthology, *Home*. Enough to immediately start collecting stories for two more. The support shown by the writing community for *Beneath* has been no less warm, and I deeply appreciate every single one of you who submitted stories and spread the word. With such a strong community behind us, I have no doubt we will continue to grow and support authors in every way we can.

Much love,

Antonia

COMING SOON FROM GHOST ORCHID PRESS

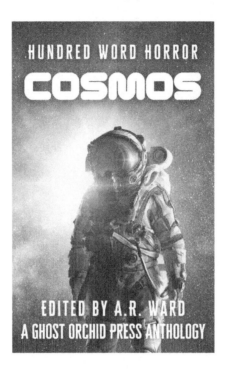

Enjoyed this book? You won't have to wait long for more Hundred Word Horror.

COSMOS: LAUNCHING MAY 2021

https://ghostorchidpress.com

Printed in Great Britain
by Amazon

61169963R00078